For "T"

First U.S. edition 2002

Library of Congress Cataloging-in-Publication Data

Heap, Sue, date.
What shall we play? / Sue Heap. —1st U.S. ed.
p.   cm.
Summary: Lily May and her friends have fun
pretending to be trees, cars, cats, Jell-O, and fairies.
ISBN 0-7636-1685-0
[1. Play—Fiction. 2. Imagination—Fiction.] I. Title.
PZ7.H34465   Wh2002
[E]—dc21   2001029511

2 4 6 8 10 9 7 5 3 1

Printed in Hong Kong

This book was typeset in 'ela' Tapioca Semi-Bold.
The illustrations were done in acrylics, wax crayons, and pencil crayon.

Candlewick Press
2067 Massachusetts Avenue
Cambridge, Massachusetts 02140

visit us at www.candlewick.com

What Shall We Play?

Sue Heap

CANDLEWICK PRESS
CAMBRIDGE, MASSACHUSETTS

"Let's play fairies," said Lily May.

"No, let's play trees," said Matt.

Matt was a big tree.

Martha was a shaky tree.

Lily May was a quiet tree.

Then all three of them were a row
of trees reaching for the sky.

"Now let's play fairies," said Lily May.

"NO," said Matt, "because we're going to play ..."

Matt
was a
bumpy
car.

Lily May
was a
new car.

Martha
was a
fast car.

Then all three of them were beep-beep cars in a traffic jam.

"Now let's play fairies," said Lily May.

Martha was a slow cat.

Matt was a sleepy cat.

Lily May was a creeping cat.

Then all three of them were noisy cats, meowing and washing their whiskers.

"Now we're going to be wibbly-wobbly Jell-O," said Matt.

And they were.

"NOW let's play fairies," said Lily May. "I have a magic wand!"

"Yes, fairies!" said Martha.

"We can all fly," said Matt.

ABRACADABRA!

All three of them
were fairies and
they could fly.